Essays

on
Education,
Literacy
and
Culture

Edited by
Tzu Yu Allison Lin

Acknowledgements

I want to thank Mr. Michael Song, the President of Showwe publishing house (Taipei, Taiwan), for his great support and his encouragement for getting academic writings published in Taiwan. Also, my thanks go to Ms. Irene Cheng, Ms. Lestat Yin, and the whole editorial team of Showwe.

Essays on Education, Literacy and Culture

Preface

In the Turkish context, how can one see the relations among key concepts such as education, literature and culture? Thinking about Turkey and comparing it to Europe or to Asia, one realises that Turkey is non of them -- and yet, Turkey is also all of them. It represents a vision in a way which it is not specifically inclusive or exclusive. It does not take everything in. But if it takes something in, it gives a new form to that -- and because of that, the way of thinking about education, literature and culture will never be the same.

The current condition is a changeable one -- both in the field of education and in the field of culture. Literature is the mediating force not only between abilities of reading and writing, but also between the self and the world, between the inner reality and its external material environment. The readers of this book will realise and will appreciate the insights that the authors have shown in their writings.

Allison Lin

Gaziantep 2022

· Contents ·

Essays on Education, Literacy and Culture

1

Culture and Religion

Adesanya M. Alabi

The relationship between Western civilization and Islam has been a very tough ideological issue, debated by many scholars. This issue has always been presented as an opinion rather than using it to bring enlightenment. In many conversational exchanges, everyone feels his or her opinions are the best, while others' are incorrect. Of course, there are going to be disagreements at some point in the knowledge presentation, but the truth is that it does not matter how divergent the ideas might be, there should be a way of enlightening the public space. With regards to this, this study explores the conflict and distinction between Western Civilization and Islam. Thus, due to some problematic issues that revolve around religious violence in recent times; from the cultural frame of reference this conflict has increased rapidly, and Islam seems to have become a scapegoat in the hands of the West.

Talking about the concept of the clash between the Western world and Islam implies that there will be a discussion about the clash that has occurred and, of course, is still occurring between Islam and the West. However, several studies have been carried out regarding this essential but delicate subject, yet there are many aspects of this clash that have not been attended to.

Looking at this concept from a contemporary point of view, one will descry that Islam has become an aunt sally to which every violent ideology is attributed. If we look at what is happening across the globe, some groups of Islam that claim to be fighting for the practice of old Islam have allowed it to become a scapegoat for those who feel or claim Islam is not compatible with Western values and its existence is egregious to global security.

In the media today, there are many examples of extremist groups that have sprung up, and their religious ideologies have egregiously caused a lot of damage to the image of Islam. For this reason, the West has become very concerned with contemporary Islam, and all the pictures they present to the entire world about Islam are negative and damaging to the precept of Islam.

Regarding the clash of civilizations, there have been many postulations by scholars. Many scholars for example, explain many of the problems that the world faces today as a result of conflicts among civilizations (Khan, 2016, p. 2). It would be appropriate to divide the nations based on their civilizations and cultures rather than group them based on their economic and political strength. These "[…] civilizations include Western, Confucian, Japanese, Islamic, Hindu, Slavic-Orthodox, Latin American and possibly African civilizations, of which the conflict between the Christian West and Islam gets the lion's share of his attention" (Khan, 2016, p. 2). In this view, this

study explores the contention between the West and Islam --
drawing from their cultural and religious worldviews. The origin
of the contention and how the clash has become irresolvable in
connection to the conflict between the Christian West and Islam
over the years are brought under focus.

Due to the fact that there is an emergence of Islam in the
global chronicle, centuries after the inception of Christian faith,
there have been many factors that are shaping the Western views
about Islam for many years. It has constantly been a critical topic
for Western writers. This "issue has been debated within the field
of international relations as a myth of the Islamic threat. This

traditional approach views Islam as the next real enemy of the post-cold war period" (Baile, 2010, p. 3).

As Islam began to experience success immediately after the Arabs had conquered the Byzantine territories, Spain began to present some religious and political issues to the Christians in which they painted Islam as a religion of violence. Western Christians did not, in the first place, quickly accept the notion that Islam is a starting point of doctrinal contention. Previously, the concept they had of Islam was just the disparity between Christian and Muslim societies, with some cultural and political absorptions. So, Islam was described as a religion with just a mere tribal disparity, and it became a subject of dispute about Christian values.

The western concept of Islam has not been critically proven but has been established based on what they think and feel about Islam. During the mediaeval period, the Christians faced some problems due to the political inadequacies and the inability of the Christians to live up to the standard of their credo concept. Western Christian writers projected Islam as an instrument of violence (Esposito, 2015, p. 1068).

During the crusades, Christian historians called "Saracens" pagans who offered worship to the sun-god and

Muhammad instead of identifying them as people who also had a strict belief in monotheism. With the emergence of the Protestant Reformation and the Counter Reformation, Islam's character changed from the way the crusaders portrayed it. This accentuates the digression in theology, false teaching, and corrupt practice -- and this was the similar allegation that Catholics and Protestants leveled against one another. As the period of enlightenment emerged, a new type of Islamic sequence was springing up. This time it was termed irrational, toxic, violent, and unfit to stand with real faith in freedom.

In recent times, the Islamic credo has been described as

a tool used to subjugate women, incite radicalism and terrorist behavior. This concept has been primarily attributed to a 20th century Protestant revolution to support literal biblical analysis. This concept continues to develop as Islam begins to go through serious persecution because it is regarded as domineering and violent. According to Western ideology, the image of Western Muslims is seen differently because of political and cultural situations. Before the West expanded itself in the contemporary era, Islamic scholars did not have a broad knowledge of the "Western Other" and also did not have much relationship with their Western neighbors.

As the previous concept of Islam was influenced by bad security system coupled with religious and political problems, the recent concept of Islam on the western border emerged through political versatility and cultural conviction. There are several questions that might come up along the line as this study progresses: How does the Western culture influence the Muslim world? How does the West present and represent Islam? What position does the West place Muslims in the modern world? How does Western culture override eastern-Islamic culture? Has Eurocentric views been an impact on Islamic credo? All these and many more are the questions that might arise in the process of the study. Furthermore, the rationality of Western cultural development and the issue of cross-cultural transposition are core issues in this aspect.

Many countries in the Islamic world that were colonized by Western powers went through some backlash. There were some clashes of identities due to the fact that Islamic societies were not properly represented by the West. There have been many conflicts that have made Islam to be misrepresented over the years. Many articles of faith and interreligious discourses have been written by western scholars that do not accurately represent Islam, and this is where problems begin to emerge and the term

Islamphobia begins to generate several topics among western writers. This obsession with identifying the "necessary enemy" or making sense of what will happen in the post-Cold War period can be seen in his work, as well as in Francis Fukuyama's *The End of History* (Baile, 2010, p. 4). Halliday tries to dispute this concept of creating a "necessary enemy." He postulates that "Western society as a whole and Western capitalism in particular have never needed an enemy in some systemic sense" (Halliday, 1996, p. 113).

The West dominated the Arab World, especially the Middle East and North Africa, and the identity of culture and religion became a serious issue. There has been a serious conflict between the Islamic cultural setting and Western ideology. From this angle, one can identify the conflict between two opposing cultures. Islamic society tries as much as possible to stick to its tradition as it has been written and mandated by the Islamic ordinances and rules. But Western culture is in sharp contrast with Islamic precepts. One crucial point to recognize here is that the West invaded the Islamic world, as they did in other parts of the world, and imposed their ideology upon the people without considering the consequence. This system can be described as one that tends to westernize the invaded territories. In this sense, the issue of trying to dominate and dehumanize the invaded environment has become a crucial issue.

The Islamic world has regarded Islam not only as a religion, but also as culture and tradition. Islam represents the Muslim world and the Muslim world represents Islam-any attempt to create a disparity might be too chaotic. The Western perspective presumably misrepresents Islam and the Muslim world. Most of the books and articles that come from the West project the Islamphobia picture to the world, and this has really been bringing a sharp disparaging remarks and feelings towards Islam.

However, one cannot absolutely pass the blame on the West

because the segregation and doctrinal differences that create some conflicts within Muslim society have also been the major weapons through which the Western writers have been using to accentuate the negative aspects of Islam. This has really caused negative perception of Islam globally. For this reason, people see Islam, which is professed to be the religion of peace, as a religion that is full of aggression, domination, and terrorism.

Another effective factor that really makes Islam a target for serious criticism is the 9/11 incident. It definitely did great damage to the image of Islam. Although people mostly attribute terrorist activities to Islam, this is due to the fact that Western writers do not positively present the image of Islam in their texts; for the fact that there have been inceptions of different sectarian groups with egregious Islamic tenet capable of dominating and terrorizing their environment. However, the readership of Western literature creates many issues regarding Islamic image and practices. On the issue of terrorism, some sects have carried out some heinous crimes, in which they attribute to Islamic principles and practices.

Nonetheless, Edward Said's *Orientalism* plays a significant role in the way Middle Eastern countries are portrayed. The author explains the efficacy of Orientalism in line with the way the West represents or misrepresents "the East" -- the social and demographical orders of those who live in Asia, the Middle East, and North Africa. The *Orientalism* therefore explains the manner in which the Arab people and their culture are presented to the world and a comparison is made with the cultural phenomenon of the West and the United States of America. In other words, this theory projects Arabian culture as barbaric, bohemian, perilous, and backward (Said, 1978, p. 73).

However, over the years, there have been a large number of Muslims pervading the West, and the West tends to dominate the Arab world through their economic and political power. Also, the

Arab world exchanges their oil for Western culture that seems to be antagonistic. The Muslims do not agree that the Western culture should override the Islamic principle in which Islam is intended to be secularized or modernized. There is a kind of cultural conflict that seems to have been creating more problems.

The Western culture believes that there is a need for secularism, logical reasoning and rationality to establish personal and collective goals while the precept of Islam places emphasis on justice and tradition as the main frame of reference of a true communal and family life. The "violence and media images has kindled a wave of interest in Europe's past and present relations with Islam" (Berger, 2014, p. 13).

Said explains intensively that *Orientalism* seriously gives a description of the disparity between the West and the Orient, their theories, social orders, literary pieces, and political record of the Orient, tradition, norms, ideology, religion, and destiny. As a result, *Orientalism*, as the case may be, allows the Eurocentric justification of colonization of the Orients in accordance with the West's self-opinionated or distorted history of the East. It presents the East as inferior to the West, and therefore, there is a need for the West to come for the liberation of the East. In this sense, the West sees themselves as superior to the people they have subjugated. Instances of *Orientalism* in its early stages can be found in European verse paintings and pictures, as well as depictions of World's Fairs in the United States of America in the 19th and 20th centuries.

The image created by European artists in the 19th and the 20th centuries establishes the early historical picture of the Orientalist phantom that has pervaded the common tradition of the understanding of the East. As we all know today, the image of Islam is being damaged across the globe due to the fact that there have been different sects of Islam that misrepresent Islam and also misinterpret its precept for their own selfish gratification. In this sense, there are many people in this contemporary dispensation who feel and think that the ideology behind Islam is violent, thus there is a need for a reform even as Christianity also went through a process of reforms.

As it has become obvious that the world is degenerating and many unnatural phenomena are emerging in different parts of the world, there are many ideological developments in Islam which have caused a great distinction among the Islamic scholars and faithful. Everyone reads and interprets the Holy Quran in different ways of understanding and interpretation. The following questions require answers: who are the self-acclaimed custodians of the Islamic faith? How do they control people's minds? What is the motive behind their doctrines? What are the features that make their studies encourage religious misconduct and extremism? How do they present and represent Islam to their followers? How do their followers accept their precepts, and how do they propagate their precepts to others? From this vintage point, there are different ways in which people interpret the Quran -- and this could have been what has created major concern and conflict in the Muslim community.

Learning about Islam is very important. In order to understand the efficacy of Islamic creed, the principles entailed in being a responsible Muslim, and the reason one must maintain these principles permanently is taught.

There has been indoctrination from different sects of Islam. Some of them teach what Islam does not really represent. Islam encourages learning, but the question is: how do we learn? From whom do people learn? Why do we learn? How do we apply what we learn? In this sense, we must admit that education is different from indoctrination in Islam. Islamic education teaches morals, kindness, and generosity.

Education usually has a positive intent. It is meant to establish knowledge and enlightenment in people's minds. In contrast, indoctrination is always used for negative means, and it always yields negative results. In Islam, Muslims are not permitted to be indoctrinated but to be educated in the way the prophet of Islam has set the examples. The Islamic extremists never present these cogent elements of the Islamic credo on this sensitive subject. Many discourses "often saw 9/11 as a full-scale assault on the global hegemony of America, in particular, and a reaction by Islamic fundamentalists against Western culture, in general" (Norris, 2002, p. 2).

Looking at the different categories of civilizations that are indicated, the clash between the West and Islam, as postulated by Edward Said, attracts the attention of Huntington. As he tries to identify the blood-spattered situation in this conflicting issue-minor conflict (local) and major conflict (global), there is a concept that the conflict between the West and "others", specifically between the West and Islam, is on minimal and major levels. Hence, the "...incidents of 9/11, attacks in Paris on November 13, 2015, and San Bernardino shooting of December 2, 2015, endorsed the Clash of Civilisations theorists" (Khan, 2016, p. 16).

To recognize the conflict between Muslims and non-Muslims demonstrates that Islam and Western culture are incompatible, particularly in modern life and democratic politics. Therefore, the possibility of peaceful coexistence between Muslims and the West is without tranquility. But looking at those instances indicated as the causes of the clashes between the West and Islam, it becomes clear that the conflict is a fundamental one in as much as cultural disparity is involved.

One will ask if those examples mentioned about the conflicts between Arabs and Jews in Palestine, Indians and Pakistanis, and Sudanese Muslims and Christians, among others, are solely or primarily religiously motivated. (Baile, 2010, p. 10). In fact, in this sense, politics has played a significant role in this situation. This approach is not reliable because it has some political undertones. The political elements of the clash are not taken seriously, but the religious components are highly dignified. However, Khan explains that:

> While dividing the world into major civilisations, the clash between Islam and the Christian West appears to be a concern for the policy makers in the West and is much-debated subject in the subsequent writings on civilizational conflicts. The series of historical conflicts between Islam and the West or to be more specific Christianity have

come to occupy an extremely large space in the memories about the centuries-old relationship. The existing clash between the two in one form or the other takes us back to the history of Jihad and Crusades (Khan, 2016, p. 6).

The function of Islam is, therefore, on several occasions, utilized to serve sinister intention; it is either to hold on to a political power for a long period of time or to canonize or demonize a political position (Hunter, 1998, p. 168). As a result, if conflict is fundamentally based on the pursuit of a religious orbital road, the Christian faith should not be ignored in the

Western world. For instance, the Christian faith strictly kicks against homosexuality, premarital sexual activity, and even having a child without marriage -- these are strictly not permitted in Western Christian doctrines.

Also, many Western Christians are critical about abortions, irrespective of what the reason for the abortion may be, because they believe that no man is permitted to take someone else's life except God. So, Western Christians have some issues that create conflicts. With regards to this, it is not only Muslims that have conflict. With Western values, Western Christians also have problems with Western secularism. Therefore, the prediction of conflict is not only possible among civilizations, but also within them. This is a cogent point that should be put into consideration.

To sum up, talking about the clash between the West and contemporary Islamic society, it means there is a cultural disparity, there is a distinction of norms and tradition between two opposing civilizations. Their belief system and way of life are not compatible, and this can always create schism. This has become a very tough ideological issue which is being deliberated every time among scholars. And this ideological issue is dealt with in a way that everyone proves to be right while the others are wrong. Hence, what is more important about this issue is how researchers, intellectuals, and scholars create knowledge rather than opinions in the public space.

Considering this position from the behavior of some extremists, one may think this is the case; it is likely the complex reality. But the most important thing is that one needs to understand the efficacy of the diversity of Muslim groups and the way individuals deal with culture. For instance, some Muslim groups use Islam as a radical political tool, and they present themselves as the foes of democracy, Western values, equality between men and women, and innovation. But if one considers the way Islam is operated in different contexts, one will understand that it has respect for Western values.

Islamphobia has become a serious concept in the anti-Islam discourse, and this has beclouded the judgment of many scholars in recent times. In this regard, several debates over the Quran have evolved, and many politicians are becoming vocal in their disdain for Islam in a way that has not been experienced before, even after 9/11. In the course of discussing the causes of this, it is essential to remember that Westerners and Americans have become more vulnerable than ever after 9/11.

This has really influenced how Westerners and Americans see the world and how they see themselves in it. For this obvious and identifiable reason, Islam has become a scapegoat for the West. However, looking at this issue from the critical point of view, one will realize that the current disparagement against Islam serves a political purpose, but it is not a wise concept because any kind of demonization against Islam fosters tensions within the Muslim community.

It is eventually counter-productive; it is essential to understand that the universality of Islam does not mean its uniformity, but the common principle that unites it. With regard to this, there is a common principle of accepting the diversity of Islamic interpretations -- that is, one Islam and many interpretations.

References

Baile, M. W. (2010). In the Name of Civilization: Islam versus the West: Term Paper for MAS in Peace and Conflict Transformation World Peace Academy (WPA). Basel, Switzerland.

Berger, M. S. (2014). *A Brief History Of Islam In Europe: Thirteen Centuries Of Creed, Conflict And Coexistence.* Leiden University Press.

Halliday, Fred, (1996). *Islam & the Myth of Confrontation*, New York: I.B. Tauris.

Hunter, S. (1998). *The Future of Islam and the West: Clash of Civilizations or Peaceful Coexistence*, Westport: Praeger.

Khan, M. (2016). Is a Clash between Islam and the West Inevitable?. *Strategie Studies* Vol. 36, No. 2 (Summer 2016), 1-23.

Said, E. (1978). *Orientalism.* New York: Vintage.

2

Humanity

Andre Shih

What matters is humanity. The conversation between Allison Lin and I is always on this topic with a diversity of articles. These articles are about physical science, biology, neurology, psychoanalysis, sociology, geopolitics, economics, music, art, film and literature, and they are all making us think about the meaning of humanity.

Natural science and humanity are linked. Physics gives us different points of view. For example, we have known about light. Without light, we simply cannot see. It's obvious. No explanations are needed. Even recent studies of relativity and quantum mechanics which are primarily concerned with light, it seems that light is still mysterious. For example, two quantum systems separated by an arbitrary distance are linked. According to Serge Haroche, this cannot be explained by classical physics.

Recent studies of relativity and quantum mechanics do not agree with classical physics. In some ways, it shows the beauty of science. Science only tells the truth, and it cannot be hidden or changed. Science tells us how Nature works, and we study Nature for our life interests. Without Nature, we cannot survive. With Nature, we develop culture in order to live as human beings. It is impossible to know all the secrets about how Nature comes to work. We study it to get to know each other and we learn skills for our survival.

Neurology is another example that researches and studies can help us understand our relationship with Nature. Studies on our brain show that emotions are our instincts that have been guiding our primitive life for a long time. We lived in a world and "our resources were of a social nature" according to Robin Dunbar, anthropologist and professor emeritus of evolutionary psychology at Oxford. "Fear, joy, sadness, disgust and shame marked the importance of social integration for our species."

Great feelings are tools for bonding with others, which will "help our genes carry on." It is a powerful and also instinctive engine. If we see our basic instincts with our contemporary civilization, we find them wild. But these "wild" instincts guarantee our survival from circles.

These instincts continue to serve us. Yet with the onset of technology, some of us live only by our wild instincts. They seem to be going down several steps on the ladder of civilization. Our basic instincts guide us through "primitive" spaces of the Internet. Our instincts and the Internet are tools. They are neither harmful nor beneficial. Our instincts tell us when we want to do things and what action we should take. But with the Internet, it gives us a different feeling. The Internet makes one seem closer than one is offline because one is able to comment or send messages to other internet users. It robs us of our ability to "feel" the true distance between people.

Not only do we have more "direct" feelings with the appearance of the Internet, but we react in a different way. We need to stimulate our brains through social interactions in order for them to develop. Yet this social interaction is changing with the Internet. It is more passive. For example, it is agreed that the baby learns a language with the real interaction between his parents and his surroundings. But it was assumed that a child can learn a language by spending a lot of time watching videos on the Internet. It is a passive way of learning because the brain only passively receives things.

Besides, it can happen to adults and the result is worse.

When we spend a lot of time looking at the screen, it prevents us from thinking deeply and questioning. As a result, we no longer know who or what to believe. We get used to repetitive and mechanical things that can make us feel relaxed and confident. If life were as simple as a multiple-choice quiz, it would be very boring.

Media would only be useful if we knew how to use it. Otherwise, it would be a burden, and we will become slaves of that burden. We have technology that renews itself with unprecedented speed, and it is in our daily lives. Yet we are on the verge of forgetting to be human. We lose our senses in common, our instincts, our feelings and our know-how to express.

We find ourselves stupid, violent and pathetic. It is as if civilization is degrading. The most important thing is to keep the ability to think deeply and actively. It is not shameful to be impulsive, but it is better to react after reflection. Technology is useful only when we know our instincts well. Man can survive without technology, but we cannot exist without Nature.

Basic things are often essential like light in the universe and feelings in social integration and also money in the economic system. This affects all of us. Because of the pandemic, we have experienced a drop in global GDP. The amount of debt is rising, and we are entering an era of over-indebtedness. That is, to pay the debt with the debt. Over-indebtedness is a problem, and it is horrifying. You can't pretend to be blind. This problem needs to be solved. The debts will be repaid otherwise the investors will no longer lend.

Nevertheless, the State continues to borrow. As the theory has it, a sovereign State can free itself from the constraints of the deficit and the debt since it controls the monetary emission. And yet, the consequence of indebtedness is that the sleeping monster of inflation will eventually wake up.

When we look at the situation in the EU, the indebtedness between countries is different. Since 2010, the German public debt has stopped increasing. It decreased from 80% to 60% before the health crisis. That of France is, on the contrary, increasing. Divergence is growing, risking a fiscal crisis in the EU. How will the European Central Bank hold its monetary policy? Because it is based on the system, in which all members of the EU must agree with each other. Therefore, if any of them were to oppose, it would be a disaster for the EU and it would have significant impacts to the whole world.

Are there any solutions? Instead of capitalism, we have

other economic systems, and they could free us from the financial crisis. Marx's theory could be a way out. Green finance, a new kind of economy, perhaps would be another. Green finance collects money from everyone to invest in infrastructure projects. It highlights the general interest, the social bond and the improvement of the living conditions of the populations. You could say it is a method of using capitalist powers to deliver public services. It's not like traditional finance. However, there are doubts about this too. If there were risks in countries -- such as unstable political situations, would they invest? Even if there were criticisms, it is good to know that there is a possible method to make capitalism and socialism work together. In any case, there is no system that can last forever. We need to have a bit of eclecticism and observe how the world will change.

And the world is changing fast. Since 2020, there are many changes. When we thought that the health crisis and the economic fall were the last, Russia attacked Ukraine in early 2022. Thousands of people died. Yet it is not the worst war. The story repeats itself. There is always some sort of war. What could we learn, except for the death and madness of the human beings?

An archaeological research in 2019 is trying to find the body of a general who led the Battle of Valutino, a confrontation between France and Russia in 1812. The search got off to a bad start. The researchers only found the bullets at the end. We have no news from archaeology. But this research makes us think about these questions: What would happen if they found the general's bone? Would the researchers rewrite history? How important is a body to us? The war is over. One cannot reincarnate 10,000 dead souls in Valutino. If they were alive, what would they care about the present and our society?

According to Tolstoy, in his novel *War and Peace*, he thinks that the Franco-Russian war in 1812 is "the wish" of all the French and all the Russians because, without them, Napoleon could not have done it against Alexander I. So it's because of madness. Ironically, it's the same madness that you fight for money or for a bottle of wine. We spend so much time fighting. One should feel ashamed for immature acts. What one can do in this world is "to love life even in pain" as Tolstoy said.

After the war, people suffer. It is easy for them to fall for revenge and the terrorists manipulate them by their feelings. Terrorists could have a chance in the battles, as they redefine justice in their way. But the loss of the loved ones or of freedom is never a reason to start another war. A war brings us loss and suffering. There is never any sort of winner. And then, hate reminds hate and we can't get out of this circle of revenge. If we don't let revenge take us, we can regain a normal life and freedom. Even if one can't reincarnate the dead, one can still reconcile with oneself. We can free ourselves from resentment, which allows us to live in peace again.

It seems that we live in a more primitive world, comparing to our ancestors. We live in an era of pandemic; therefore, the priority is to stay alive every day. We often argue because of the economic crisis. We wage war without talks. If we traveled back in time, there was a time when there was no war and we had plenty of money. People lived without fear and the media was still cute.

It's the 1920s where the bohemian generation lived -- crazy, drunk and lost. In Hemingway's writing, the city of Paris is like a Party. Paris was a big city where many writers and artists met. Either they were poor or romantic. Either they are rich or rigid. One evening followed another. Crazy love, alcoholic intellectual, beautiful Jazz music were their life. It was also in Paris where Hemingway chose to start his career and where he met people like Picasso. And then he thundered with the authority of success. The 1920s, indeed, were the glamour of the 20th century.

And yet, we are not them and they are not us. Is it the

heroes who create a new glorious period? Or is it the current of time that is favorable for ordinary people to become the hero? Perhaps heroes and timing are the two essential elements for civilization to achieve its so-called Golden Age.

We know their life through metaphors in literature. The writers are sensitive to the political and artistic movements. They use metaphor to describe good and bad with their point of view. It allows us to see the story in a profound perspective and we can understand better what was going on. As the use of metaphors is dazzling, it is a clue to understand this very period.

Literature and art not only show us life in the past, but also make us hope for the future. In literature or in other forms of art, such as film, music or painting, there are of course humanitarian messages. These messages help us to live in hope. When we see a work of art, we have an understanding and we have a reflection.

We could have a new idea and we could find a way out of our problems. For example, when the Black Lives Matter movement happened in the United States, it was the perfect time to watch the movie *Gone with the Wind*. Many of the parts in the movie touches our heats, as they show the hard time which people went through, no matter they are black or white, male or female.

All lives matter -- it is not just about black people, or just about the human beings. If we ignore the importance of life, we risk not getting along with others or even with Nature. So, after knowing the messages in the forms of art, it is possible for us to find a way out.

Art can give us hope. Moreover, art can also heal us. An exercise created by Jung is to let go and to play like a child. This is art therapy. Imagination can also heal us. We connect the conscious and the unconscious, healing the wound by playing with our imagination. By playing, painting, or simply talking, we reactivate our memories. Thus, the "modification" and "transformation" of the image are possible. That is how we regain self-power and reduce the symptoms of trauma.

In addition, the game allows us to reconnect with our childhood. Above all, "everything is possible in a game." We integrate our experience with our reality, so that we don't run away from our suffering but transform it to a level of understanding and acceptance. In a society of crisis, one can still find the healing power in arts, in order to embrace life.

3

Ideology

Connie Au, Burcu Asiltürk

This research aims to present a contextual analysis of the key ideological symbols in *Fahrenheit 451*. It also looks into the way in which symbolism in the literary text relates to the themes of censorship and ideology. Althusser's theory of ideology is used to explain the ideological status and censorship. These symbols are read to see how they affect knowledge longevity, freedom, and survival.

The dystopian society in the novel *Fahrenheit 451* is demonstrated as a place of uncertainties lacking of personal rights and humanity. The authority deploys ideology for survival and a range of technologies to maintain control and expects citizens to conform.

Guy Montag, the novel's main protagonist, is a fireman, and in this society, firemen set fires rather than extinguish them

(Smolla, 2009, p. 896). He, along with the other firemen, is responsible for destroying the books by burning them (Gebreen, 2020, p. 215). They serve as the authorized protector of the society keeping citizens away from the "dangers" (Smolla, 2009, p. 895). But the definition of being in danger is ironically wrong and different from the reader's common understanding.

Montag later realizes that the authority is attempting to limit people's freedom and control their conscience after encountering a "crazy seventeen" (Bradbury, 2008, p. 14) girl named Clarisse. He then begins to doubt his task, questioning why firemen are required to set fires and destroy books (Gebreen, 2020, p. 215).

He knows that "he was not happy" (Bradbury, 2008, p. 20) and recognizes "the true state of affairs" (Bradbury, 2008, p. 20). He stops destroying books and starts reading them.

Bradbury makes significant use of symbolism throughout the book to mirror the dystopian side of real society and how the government employs ideology and severe censorship to control its citizens' mentalities and sustain the dystopian system shown in this novel. These symbols, unfortunately, represent the suppression of the ideas, the danger of censorship, and the implications of total government control (Gebreen, 2020, p. 216). His repetitive use of symbols also adds to the drama and the futuristic setting in which he portrays the truth, as the following sections would show.

The Mechanical Hound is the first symbol in the novel. The Mechanical Hound, a robotic dog, has been programmed by the government. It is capable of tracking, hunting, and killing the person who keeps books (as books are seen illegal).

The Hound symbolizes the government's manipulation:

Come off it. It doesn't like or dislike. It just "functions". It's like a lesson in ballistics. It has a trajectory we decide for it. It follows through. It targets itself, homes itself, and cut off. It's only copper wire, storage batteries, and electricity. (Bradbury, 2008, p. 38).

[...] Mechanical Hound never fails. Never since its first use in tracking quarry has this incredible invention made a mistake. (Bradbury, 2008, p. 171).

In the text, the Mechanical Hound symbolizes the government's eyes, and keeps an eye on people. It is constantly looking for opportunities to attack. The Hound is a symbol of repressive state apparatus. According to Althusser, his theory of ideology indicates that the State can be seen "as a repressive apparatus" (Althusser, 1994, p. 106), which is functioning through different forms of ideology -- namely, through "the system of the ideas and representations which is dominate the mind of a man or a social group" (Althusser, 1994, p. 120).

Throughout the novel, the firemen use the Hound to track down rule-breakers and criminals. This implies that the Hound, like the firemen, has the capacity to identify and to punish crimes, thus enforcing the ideology imposed by the government.

In addition, the Hound acts as a deterrent to those who transgress the rules, which causes people's fear and passivity.

Montag himself too, for example, is terrified, as the dog and states threatening him with a ferocious like growl:

> Montag touched the muzzle. The Hound growled. Montag jumped back. The Hound half rose in its kennel and looked at him with green-blue neon light flickering in its suddenly activated eye-bulbs. It growled again, a strange rasping combination of electrical sizzle, a frying sound, a scraping of metal, a turning of cogs that seemed rusty and ancient with suspicion. "No, no, boy," said Montag, his heart pounding. (Bradbury, 2008, p. 36-37).

As we can see, the Mechanical Hound can identify any suspicious behaviour, such as the hiding of books. For instance, the Hound can virtually detect the change in Montag's mood. As a result, Montag is terrified, implying that the dog is capable of discouraging crime and identifying possible rebellion (Gebreen, 2020, p. 248).

In *Fahrenheit 451*, fire conveys three different meanings. Fire signifies destruction at the beginning of the story:

It was a pleasure to burn. It was a special pleasure to see things eaten, to see things blackened and changed.

With the brass nozzle in his fists, with this great python spitting its venomous kerosene upon the world, the blood pounded in his head, and his hands were the hands of some amazing conductor playing all the symphonies of blazing and burning to bring down the tatters and charcoal ruins of history. (Bradbury, 2008, p. 9).

Montag is proud of his work as a firefighter, enjoying seeing things "blackened and changed" (Bradbury, 2008, p. 9) and praising his contributions to the dominant ideology (Ersöz-Koç, 2015, p. 122). The fire represents the repressive state apparatus (Ersöz-Koç, 2015, p. 109), signifying a weapon for government's censorship and control, implying that the state's goal is cultural uniformity.

The Fire is a terrifying and a powerful destructive force and is a means of restoring societal harmony:

> They pumped the cold fluid from the numbered 451 tanks strapped to their shoulders. They coated each book, they pumped rooms full of it [...] The woman knelt among the books touching the drenched leather and cardboard, reading the gilt titles with her fingers while her

eyes accused Montag. (Bradury, 2008, p. 52).

The woman's hand twitched on the single matchstick. The fumes of kerosene bloomed up about her. Montag felt the hidden book pound like a heart against his chest. (Bradbury, 2008, p. 53).

This excerpt depicts a burning operation in the old woman's house. Since books constitute a threat to the society's ability to think critically, and instead convinces people that destroying books is in the best interests of society. Here, the firemen burn the books together with the old woman as she refuses to leave the house. This incident triggers the shift of Montag's consciousness from the old and ignorant Montag to the new Montag because of the totalitarian regime's atmosphere of censorship and dictatorship.

The Fire symbol takes a more neutral meaning when Montag comes to appreciate the use of the fire:

> And as before, it was good to burn, he felt himself gush out in the fire, snatch, rend, rip in half with flame, and put way the senseless problem [...] Fire was the best thing!

(Bradbury, 2008, p. 151).

As we can see, Montag was an obedient member of society who followed the ideologies of the government, but later he started to change. He subsequently burns down his house after discovering that he "never burned right" (Bradbury, 2008, p. 154). He sees fire as a solution, or a means of maintaining control. This suggests that he buries his artificial societal self and gives birth to himself a new intellectual life (Watt, 1980, p. 79). His transformation symbolizes both his resistance to the government and his rejection of established norms and values.

As a symbol, the Fire has a better connotation toward the end of the novel:

> The fire was gone, then back again, like a winking eye. He stopped, afraid he might blow the fire out with a single breath. But the fire was there and he approached warily, from a long way off [...] That small motion, the white and red colour, a strange fire because it meant a different thing to him. It was not burning; it was warming! (Bradbury, 2008, p. 187).

Montag is drawn to the fire and observes the fire carefully after fleeing the society in which he lives. He appreciates the real beauty of fire and feels its warmth. He even notices that the "smell was different" (Bradbury, 2008, p. 187). Here, fire represents rebirth and renewal, which has a positive connotation. For Montag, fire is no longer a destructive force, but rather a pleasant and uplifting symbol for regeneration.

The Fire also represents Montag's literal rebirth and purification. This is symbolized by the phoenix:

"What?" There was a damn silly bird called a Phoenix

back before Christ... But every time he burnt himself up he sprang out of the ashes, he got himself born all over again. (Bradbury, 2008, p. 209).

Granger, the leader of the "Book People", compares man to the mythical Phoenix. He believes that there is a destruction and rebirth cycle, as the Phoenix did. Montag, by burning his house, is similar to the phoenix in that he frees himself from the societal influences and develops his individuality.

The TV walls are also viewed as a major symbol in *Fahrenheit 451*. They appear in Montag and Mildred's living room for the first time. They have become an integral part of society's lifestyle and entertainment since the books are censored. More televisions are placed on the walls of the living room if the family's financial condition is well. Mildred, for example, has three-walled parlors in her living room and wants to "have fourth wall installed" (Bradbury, 2008, p. 30).

In the society, television is employed as a propaganda tool to influence people's minds and reinforce ideologies. This is similar to what Althusser states that the government mainly controls their citizens' perspectives through the ideological apparatuses with the use of technologies to impose order and reinforce the control of a dominant class.

Mildred's view of the television show's characters as family is the first example of ideological apparatuses:

> "How's Uncle Louis today?" "Who?" "And Aunt Maude?" The most significant memory he had of Mildred, really, was of a little girl in a forest without trees... No matter when he came in, the walls were always talking to Mildred. (Bradbury, 2008, p. 60).

> "Will you turn the parlor off?" he asked. "That's my

family." "Will you turn it off for a sick man?" "I'll turn it down." She went out of the room and did nothing to the parlour and came back [...] "That's my favourite program," she said. (Bradbury, 2008, p. 65).

The television is designed and created to influence citizens' psychology and shape specific ways of thinking. Mildred has immersed herself into the television life and is into "the family" through the medium of television. The family is a symbol of state control that pervades society via interactive television shows (Bradbury, 2008, p. 30). People spend their days interacting with their "family" or "friends" by staring at these massive wall screens in their home.

This also echoes with Baker (2005) in which he comments "The unreality shown by the television screens relates to a constructed ideology that conceals the true status of the world from its citizens" (p. 493). People are separated from the true reality, which prevents them from comprehending how their lives have been controlled and their ability to think freely severely limited. This implies that the invasion of TV parlor walls into citizens' homes could be used to supplant critical thinking (Gebreen, 2020, p. 219).

Another example of television used as a propaganda tool is when Montag is pursued by the police force. It is broadcast in real time on television:

> "Montag," the TV set said, and lit up. "M-O-N-T-A-G."
> The name was spelled out by the voice. "Guy Montag.
> Still running. Police helicopters are up. A new Mechanical
> Hound has been brought from another district... Tonight,
> this network is proud to have the opportunity to follow the
> Hound by camera helicopter as it starts on its wat to the
> target..." (Bradbury, 2008, p. 171).

[...] An announcer on the dark screen said, "The search is over, Montag is dead; a crime against society has been avenged [...]" They didn't show the man's face in focus. Did you notice? Even your best friends couldn't tell if it was you. They scrambled just enough to let the imagination take over. Hell," he whispered. (Bradbury, 2008, p. 192).

Montag manages to escape from the society in which he lives at the end of the novel. His "faking" (Bradbury, 2008, p.

190) of death is shown on television when the Hound kills him. The authority is attempting to create an illusion that he has been arrested, aiming to "let the imagination take over" (Bradbury, 2008, p. 192). This is similar to what Baker (2005) suggesting that "the spectacle of death is one that keeps the citizens pacified (or perhaps ideologically anaesthetized)" (p. 493). The readers are led to believe that it is difficult for citizens to verify information received through television or other media, implying that the government has complete control of the "truth".

Furthermore, television has an alienating influence on personal relationships:

His wife in the TV parlor paused long enough from reading her script to glance up. "Hey," she said. "The man's thinking!" "Yes," he said. "I wanted to talk to you." He paused... "you took all the pills in your bottle last night." "The bottle was empty." [...] She was quite obviously waiting for him to go. "I didn't do that," she said. (Bradbury, 2008, p. 29).

"Nobody listens anymore. I can't talk to the walls because they're yelling at me. I can't talk to my wife; she listens to

the walls. I just want someone to hear what I have to say."
(Bradbury, 2008, p. 107).

This excerpt shows that Mildred is freeing herself from the oppression of the government. Mildred is drawn to the parlour walls and television programs since they are the only stimulus in her life. She is also drawn away from her friends, and especially her husband. Mildred refuses to discuss the overdose incident with Montag. The only thing that Mildred wants is to "waiting for him to go" (Bradbury, 2008, p. 29).

Montag later expresses his opinions on television, claiming

that all he wants is to be heard. The readers seem to understand how television has harmed their relationship by creating an emotional barrier between them in this situation. Individuals value entertainment and technology more than their privacy, family life, and freedom. The role of technology is shaping society's value (Rossuck, 1997, p. 67), is to regulate the individual through media content, causing all citizens behave and, most importantly, think alike.

Bradbury highlights the sharp contrast between the ideal society and the reality, as well as the government's use of this deception to manipulate the citizens. The authority is attempting to create an illusion that he has been arrested. The readers are led to believe that it is difficult for citizens to verify information received through television or other media, implying that the government has complete control of the "truth". These examples demonstrate how the dystopian government has complete control over society and how fear is used to manipulate civilians. The consequences of defying the government are once again reminded to its people.

The society in *Fahrenheit 451* utterly pursues "cultural homogenization". The authority of the state relies on its concern about the suppression of freedom and thinking (Gebreen, 2020,

p. 219). The Hound and TV walls represent censorship to limit people the right to express themselves, to silence all the valuable sources of knowledge, and to maintain citizens through TV wall programs and the Mechanical Hound's surveillance. Montag and others recognize how these technologies hinder individuals from retrieving knowledge, thinking for themselves, criticizing, and appreciating nature. That is why they memorize books in order to keep information alive and extend knowledge longevity.

Bradbury, on the other hand, uses fire as a symbol to represent ideology for survival (destruction, a solution, and rebirth). At the beginning, firemen destroy books to limit knowledge longevity. Montag gradually realises the true state of affairs and destroys his old self to form his new self. The fire resembles Montag can think for himself again and break the government's control.

The symbols in *Fahrenheit 451* signify the government's censorship and survival ideology. The government imposes the forced conformity and restricts citizens' fundamental right by limiting their knowledge longevity. The majority of citizens are unaware that they have a choice and personal freedom. They merely conform themselves to the government's rules, losing their individuality and ability to criticize in the process.

Everyone is being pushed in one ideological direction as if it were the only way to survive. The citizens and the books can be said to be victims as a result of the censorship and survival ideology.

References

Abbasi, I. S. & Al-Sharqi, L. (2015). Media Censorship: Freedom Versus Responsibility. *Journal of Law and Conflict Resolution* 7(4), 21-25.

Althusser, L. (1994). Ideology and Ideological State Apparatuses. *Mapping Ideology*. Ed., Slavoj Žižek. London: Verso.

Bradbury, R. (2008). *Fahrenheit 451*. London: Harper Collins.

Baker, B. (2005). Ray Bradbury: *Fahrenheit 451. A Companion to Science Fiction*. Ed., David Seed, Oxford: Wiley-Blackwell.

Gebreen, H. A. K. (2020). Dystopian World of Ray Bradbury's Fahrenheit 451. *International Journal of Linguistics, Literature and Translation 3*(7), 215-222.

Ersöz-Koç, E. (2015). Subject and State: Ideology, State Apparatuses and Interpellation in Fahrenheit 451. *Belgrade English Language and Literature Studies 111*(73), 107-131.

Mumby, D. K. (2009). Ideology & the Social Construction of Meaning: A Communication Perspective. *Communication Quarterly 37*(4), 291-304.

Rossuck, J. (1997). Banned books: A Study of Censorship. *The English Journal 86*(2), 67-70.

Smolla, R. A. (2009). The Life of the Mind and a Life of Meaning: Reflections on Fahrenheit 451. *Michigan Law Review 107*(6), 895- 912.

Watt, D. (1980). Burning Bright: Fahrenheit 451 as Symbolic Dystopia. *Ray Bradbury.* Eds., Joseph Olander and M. H. Greeberg. New York: Taplinger.

Yılmaz, R. (2015). A Study of "The Other" in Ray Bradbury's Fahrenheit 451. *International Journal of Media Culture and Literature 1*(2), 27-44.

4

Utopia

Ahmet Basar, Allison Lin, Mehmet Sincar

Although the idea of Utopia indicates an imaginary place, there must be more than one place like this in the history of writing, so that we can compare one Utopia to another. In this research, the authors read the work of two important figures in the history of writing, in their own right.

William Morris, a British writer, designer and artist, and John Dewey, an American educational reformer, compares their ideas of utopia -- how can we read them and to see the similarities between them? William Morris is the author of the novel *News from Nowhere*, in which he described his version of a utopian world in detail.

On the other hand, John Dewey's ideas about educational reform were criticised, because they seemed to be unrealistic. He later embraced these criticisms and continued to express his ideas as his utopia. The authors compare these two kinds of utopia, in terms of education.

Even though they grew up and lived in different cultures, Morris' and Dewey's views seem to have a significant common ground. It is essential to show that through similarities, the readers can achieve a better understanding of their worlds.

According to *Oxford Dictionary of Literary Terms*, the word utopia means

[a] n imagined form of ideal or superior (usually communistic) human society; or a written work of fiction

or philosophical speculation describing such a society. [...]. The word was coined by Sir Thomas More in his Latin work *Utopia* (1516), as a pun on two Greek words, eutopos ("good place") and outopos ("no place"). (Baldick, 2008, p. 348).

The authors aim to compare the idea of utopia in John Dewey's and William Morris's writings, highlighting the similarities in their views. Dewey (1859 - 1952), an American philosopher, a psychologist, and an educational reformer, had significant influences in concepts on education and on social reform. Morris (1834 - 1896), a British textile designer, a poet, an artist, a novelist, an architectural conservationist, a printer, a translator, and a socialist activist associated with the British Arts and Crafts Movement, has contributed greatly to the revival of traditional British textile arts and production methods.

Morris's literary contributions helped to establish the genre of fantasy in a modern sense. He also helped to develop the ideas of socialism in England. The authors will read Morris's novel *News from Nowhere*, which portrays his interpretation of utopia and again the authors will compare this literary text to the way in which Dewey describes his utopia.

News from Nowhere, written in 1890, is a utopian romance. It is a story about the future of England. It expresses thoughts about "the good society," in a way which Morris believed in. Although the ideas of utopia before him inspired him, like Thomas More's in 1516 and Edward Bellamy's in 1888, he also criticised them for being "too medieval" and "too materialist, a mechanical vision". That is why he wrote his version of utopia in *News from Nowhere*, criticising the ideas of utopia before him and the real-world dogmas present of his time.

John Dewey's relation to the word utopia can be found in Lan T. E. Deweese-Boyd's article. For Deweese-Boyd, Dewey's vision of education can be understood as the Utopians', because for "each boy and girl", the Utopian educators want "to find out what each individual person" can do in his or her own "conditions of the environment" (Deweese-Boyd, 2015, p. 70). After that, each person will create a specific way of learning and living in the society, "shaping desires and developing needs" (Deweese-Boyd, 2015, p. 71) in order to serve the community.

In *News from Nowhere*, the readers can see that education does not need to happen in a school. "Education" means "to lead out" (Morris, 1993, p. 66). Children do not experience "a system of teaching" (Morris, 1993, p. 66). Here Morris breaks away from the traditional institutions of 19th century England. For reading and writing, children do wait "by the time they are four years old" (Morris, 1993, p. 66). Also, the way of some sort of "book-learning" (Morris, 1993, p. 66) actually refers to the reading and the writing of "poems" (Morris, 1993, p. 67), instead of language or history.

Equally important as Morris's idea of education shown in his novel, *News from Nowhere*, Dewey's educational theories are known as they open up a "new field of psychology to education" (Plagens, 2011, p. 41). The educational ideas were presented in his writings, such as *My Pedagogic Creed* (1897), *Democracy and Education* (1916).

Several themes recur throughout these writings. Dewey continually argues that education and learning are social and interactive processes, and thus the school itself is a social institution through which social reform can and should take place. In addition, he believed that students thrive in an environment where they are allowed to experience and interact with the curriculum. All students should have the opportunity to take part in their learning, so that they would have a better chance to be good individuals, in order to contribute to a society which could be as good as one could imagine.

References

Baldick, C. (2008). Oxford *Dictionary of Literary Terms*. Oxford: Oxford University Press.

Deweese-Boyd, I. T. E. (2015). There Are No Schools in Utopia: John Dewey's Democratic Education. *Education and Culture* 31. 2, 69-80.

Morris, W. (1993). *News from Nowhere and Other Writings*. London: Penguin.

Plagens, Gregory K. (2011). Social Capital and Education: Implications for Student and School Performance. *Education and Culture* 27.1, 40-64.

Essays on Education, Literacy and Culture

Contributors

Adesanya M. Alabi is doing his doctorial research at the department of English Language and Literature, Karabuk University, Turkey. His research interests are literary criticism, postcolonial literature and African literature. He is an energetic English teacher with a solid achievement in writing and publication. He is currently working on his thesis, which is about the social-political situation in Africa and the Middle East.

Ahmet İ. Başar completed his Master in the Department of Educational Administration, Faculty of Education, Gaziantep University. He is currently working on his doctoral research. He is an English teacher at Gaziantep Vicdan-Ahmet Güner Secondary School, Turkey.

Burcu Asiltürk is studying in the Department of American Culture and Literature at Hacettepe University, Turkey. Her research interests include linguistics, cultural studies, American and English literature which are related to concepts such as gender, power, ideology and knowledge.

Hong Yu Connie Au received her bachelor's degree in English Language and Literature from Hong Kong Shue Yan and completed her master degree in English teaching at Gaziantep University, Turkey. Her research interests include language teaching, literature, and cultural studies. Au has several article publications in English Language Teaching, including "Innovation in STEM Education: A Case Study of Teachers' STEM Perceptions and their Professional Competence Perceptions" and "An Analysis of the Effect of Peer and Teacher Feedback on EFL Learners' Oral Performances and Speaking Self-Efficacy Levels". She teaches at the School of Foreign

Languages, Gaziantep University, Turkey.

Allison Lin achieved her PhD in English and Comparative Literature at Goldsmiths, University of London. She teaches courses which are related to English Literature, Literature and Language Teaching in the Department of Foreign Language Education, Faculty of Education, Gaziantep University, Turkey. She is the co-editor of two academic Journals: *Journal of Narrative and Language Studies* (ISSN: 2148-4066) and *Journal of Innovative Research in Teacher Education* (ISSN: 2757-6116). Her publications are articles and books about literary criticism, visual arts and language education, including the most recent book, *The Condition of Language* (Taipei: Showwe, 2021). Her research interests are aesthetics in narrative forms, literary and cultural criticism.

Andre Chu-Cheng Shih has his BSc in Atmospheric Science at National Taiwan University. He obtained a M2 in Climate Dynamics at UPS, Toulouse, France. He is an engineer in the company of weather news in Chiba, Japan. His research interests are climate change, meteorology, French literature and language.

Mehmet Sincar is Professor in Educational Administration and Planning, Gaziantep University, Turkey. His research interests are focusing on theory and practice in educational administration, technology and leadership, school development, educational change and leaders.

語言文學類　PG2885　文學視界145

Essays on Education, Literacy and Culture

作　　　者／林孜郁（Tzu Yu Allison Lin）
責任編輯／尹懷君
圖文排版／黃莉珊
封面設計／吳咏潔

發 行 人／宋政坤
法律顧問／毛國樑　律師
出版發行／秀威資訊科技股份有限公司
　　　　　114台北市內湖區瑞光路76巷65號1樓
　　　　　電話：+886-2-2796-3638　傳真：+886-2-2796-1377
　　　　　http://www.showwe.com.tw
劃撥帳號／19563868　戶名：秀威資訊科技股份有限公司
　　　　　讀者服務信箱：service@showwe.com.tw
展 售 門 市／國家書店（松江門市）
　　　　　104台北市中山區松江路209號1樓
　　　　　電話：+886-2-2518-0207　傳真：+886-2-2518-0778
網路訂購／秀威網路書店：https://store.showwe.tw
　　　　　國家網路書店：https://www.govbooks.com.tw

2022年12月　BOD一版
定價：220元
版權所有　翻印必究
本書如有缺頁、破損或裝訂錯誤，請寄回更換

讀者回函卡